STICKMEN GUIDE TO THE SKY
– UNCOVERED

Thanks to the creative team:

Senior Editor: Alice Peebles
Consultant: Jacqueline Mitton
Fact checking: Kate Mitchell

Design: www.collaborate.agency

First published in Great Britain in 2016
by Hungry Tomato Ltd
PO Box 181
Edenbridge
Kent, TN8 9DP

Copyright © 2016 Hungry Tomato Ltd

No part of this publication may be
reproduced, stored in a retrieval
system, or transmitted in any form or
by any means, electronic, mechanical,
photocopying, recording, or
otherwise, without the prior written
permission of the copyright owner.

A CIP catalogue record for this book is
available from the British Library.

ISBN 978-1-910684-45-0

Printed and bound in China

Discover more at
www.hungrytomato.com

STICKMEN'S GUIDE TO THE SKY
— UNCOVERED

by Catherine Chambers
Illustrated by John Paul de Quay

Contents

6 .... The Sky

8 .... High in the Exosphere

10 .... Satellites in the Exosphere

12 .... Floating in the Thermosphere

14 .... Looking into Space

16 .... Bright Lights in the Mesosphere

18 .... The Calm Stratosphere

20 .... The Ozone Layer

22 .... Earth's Troposphere

24 .... Storms and Twisters

26 .... What's the Weather Like?

28 .... Fantastic Sky Facts

30 .... The Future...

31-32 .... Glossary and Index

The Sky

When we look up at the sky, we are looking through layers of gases called the atmosphere. These layers wrap around Earth like a pile of blankets, some thick and others thin. Each layer is made of a mixture of gases, covers a range of temperature and air pressure, and has a different effect on the way we live on Earth.

Exosphere
From around 600 km (375 miles)
Pressure is extremely low, gases are very thin and some escape into space. Most satellites orbit Earth here.

Thermosphere
Around 85-600 km (53-375 miles)
Gases are still thin, pressure is very low and the temperature increases with height. Bright coloured lights pulsate.

Mesosphere
Around 50-85 km (30-53 miles)
Temperatures are very cold. Meteors shoot through and burn up. The highest clouds put on a light show over the poles.

Stratosphere
Minimum 6-50 km (4-30 miles)
The tips of Earth's highest clouds reach here. A layer of ozone gases protects Earth from the Sun's harmful rays.

Troposphere
0-20 km (0-12 miles) maximum
We can breathe oxygen and plants use carbon dioxide to grow. The boundary with the stratosphere is very variable.

High in the Exosphere

This layer of very thin gases begins around 600 km (375 miles) above Earth's surface. Is it part of Earth's atmosphere? Or is it part of outer space? Scientists cannot agree! But a lot happens here.

Flying saucers? Not yet seen!

Sounding rocket

Satellite

Rocket's instrument package, or payload, for collecting data

Exosphere

Thermosphere

Mesosphere

Stratosphere

Payload with data

Sounding rocket

A sounding rocket shoots through the exosphere and beyond. Sounding rockets collect data from the atmosphere, the Sun and far-off galaxies. They also carry experiments that need weightless conditions. The instrument package on the rocket gathers and stores the information, and then parachutes back to Earth.

Power of the Sun

The Sun is a very active searing-hot star that radiates energy towards Earth. At times, the Sun emits strong blasts of UV rays (found beyond the violet end of the light spectrum), as shown here, and X-rays. These make the thermosphere below bulge up into the exosphere. The boundary between these layers is never exact, but it is more stable at some times than others.

Sun flare

Hydrogen atom

On the way to the Moon

The upper edge of the exosphere marks the end of Earth's atmosphere and the beginning of space. It is also halfway to the Moon.

Helium atom

Carbon dioxide molecule

Oxygen atom

Glowing exosphere

Pictures of Earth taken with a UV telescope show the exosphere glowing. This eerie light is called the geocorona. It is created by the Sun's UV rays reflecting off the cloud of hydrogen atoms surrounding the Earth.

Speedy gases

The exosphere's gases are mainly hydrogen atoms, with some helium and carbon dioxide. There are some oxygen atoms, too. These gases speed along curved paths, without colliding. Earth's gravity pulls down most of them towards the troposphere but the fastest zoom off into space.

Troposphere

Satellites in the Exosphere

About 2,000 artificial satellites orbit our planet at a height of about 20,000 km (12,400 miles) and above. They relay data, communication signals or images to Earth by means of antennae, and use solar power. They operate in the exosphere where they are safe from atmospheric drag, which would make them spiral down and burn up.

Satellite science

Each satellite has its own mission and instruments. Some track the paths of Earth's cyclones and wildfires, or monitor changes in ice sheets and oceans. Other satellites measure gases, such as carbon dioxide or ozone, that have important effects on our planet. Yet others are telescopes for observing planets, stars and galaxies far away.

Earth/Sun sensors

Satellite housing

Solar panel

Three, two, one…!

Satellites are launched into space mostly on rockets. They are released when they reach the right height and are travelling fast enough in orbit to remain there without falling to Earth. Some satellites orbit over the north and south poles. Others travel from east to west over the equator. A satellite's orbit can change, so very occasionally, satellites collide!

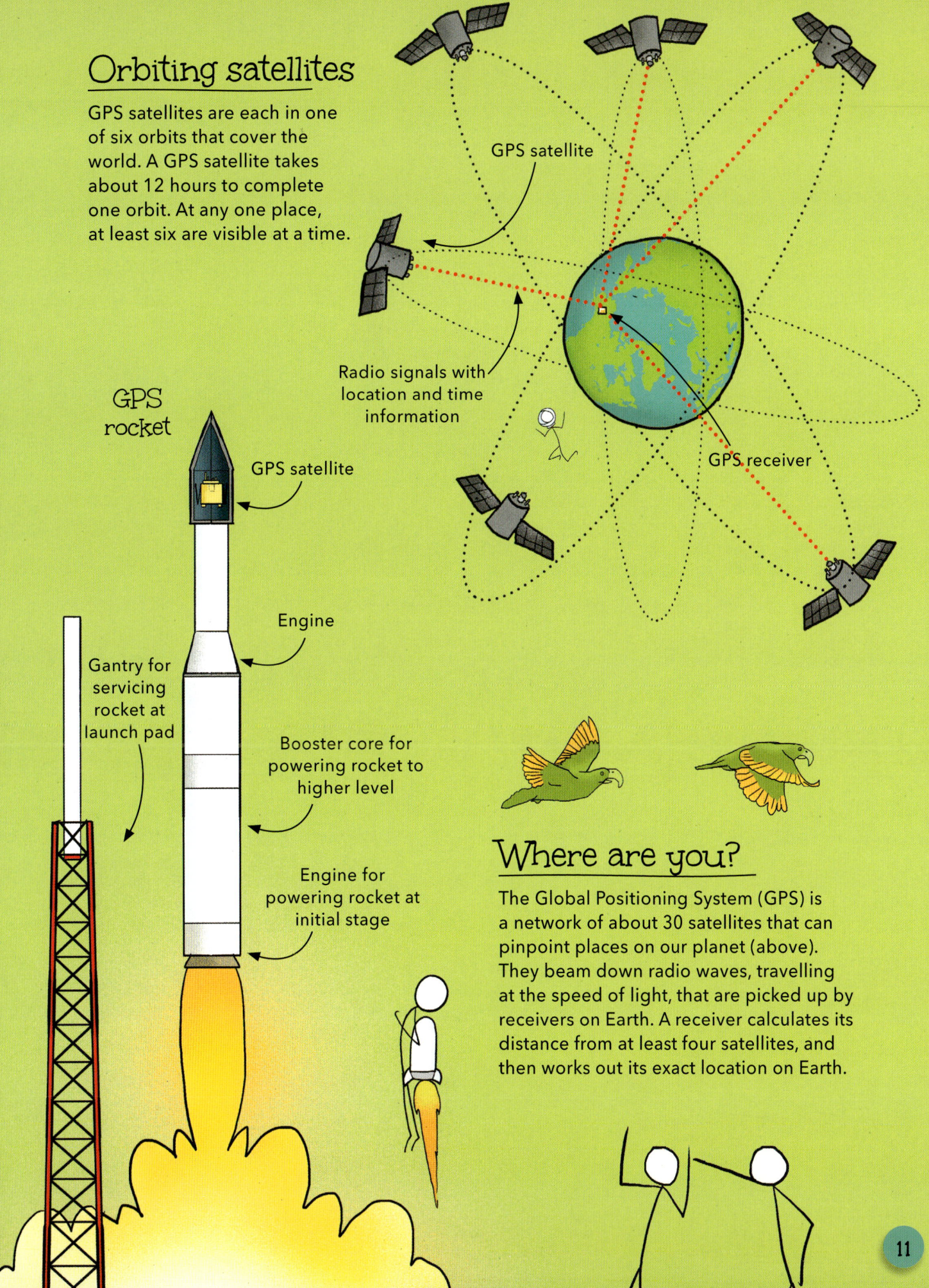

Floating in the Thermosphere

The deep thermosphere layer reaches from around 85 km (53 miles) to 600 km (375 miles) above Earth. Its main gas is nitrogen, with some oxygen, helium and hydrogen. Towards the base of this layer, temperature falls and gravity's pull is stronger.

Working together

The International Space Station (ISS) is the largest artificial object ever put in space. It orbits 320 km (200 miles) above Earth, 16 times each day. A total of 15 countries co-operated to build ISS, and astronauts from those countries spend months on board, conducting scientific experiments. The weightlessness of space brings scientific results that can be helpful to us on Earth. You can track the ISS in real time online!

Crew's research module

Double-sided solar panels provide electricity to ISS

Amazing astronauts

Astronauts are scientists and engineers trained to work inside and outside space vehicles. A spacewalk today lasts usually between five and eight hours, depending on the job to be done. Astronauts are tethered to the spacecraft to prevent them from floating away, and have a backpack with small jet thrusters to allow them to move around in space.

Oxygen line

Safety tether

One X-15 rocket plane recorded a flying height of 100 km (65 miles)

X-15 rocket plane

This experimental, hypersonic rocket-powered aircraft first flew in 1959 and still holds the speed record for a manned, powered aircraft. It reached 7,274 km/h (4,520 mph) and Neil Armstrong was one of its pilots.

External fuel tank

Super space shuttle

The space shuttle, in operation from 1982 to 2011, was the only manned, winged aircraft that could move into orbit and back again, returning its crew and payload. Its robotic arm, the Canadarm, was used to fix the ISS. It also took hold of the Hubble Space Telescope (see page 14) so that repairs could be made.

Two rocket boosters provide 71 per cent of thrust needed for launch

Orbiter (the only shuttle component that goes into orbit)

Looking into Space

The Hubble Space Telescope orbits Earth in the thermosphere at about 547 km (340 miles) above Earth. For more than 25 years, it has beamed back spectacular images of space, including planets, comets, exploding stars, nebulae (gas and dust clouds) and galaxies. Scientists use Hubble's data and images to learn more about these objects and the whole universe.

Through the telescope

Hubble captures its amazing images using both visible light and radiation we cannot see: ultraviolet and infrared, at either end of the light spectrum. It has five different instruments with cameras for taking particular kinds of images. Some of them can split light into its different wavelengths and some take pictures through special filters.

Southern Pinwheel

This is Hubble's view of a spiral galaxy, nicknamed the Southern Pinwheel, in the constellation Hydra. Lying 15 million light years away, it is relatively near and easier to see. The swirling blues and pinks are glowing gas where stars are being born. Among the thousands of star clusters and individual stars in this galaxy are supernova remnants – traces of giant stars that have exploded and died.

Pictures in the dark

Hubble has no flashlight to take images in the darkness of space. Instead, it aims and fixes on to its target with its Pointing Control System, which uses three special instruments called Fine Guidance Sensors. Then, its primary mirror captures and concentrates the light from space, reflecting it on to a smaller secondary mirror. This mirror focuses the light on to one of the cameras or instruments.

Bright Lights in the Mesosphere

The mesosphere is a thin layer of mixed gases around 50 km (30 miles) to 85 km (53 miles) above Earth. With fewer air molecules to absorb the sun's radiation, temperatures near the upper mesosphere plunge to –90°C (–130°F), the coldest in our atmosphere. Meteors shoot into this layer and then burn up.

Elve halo

Meteor from space burning up

Red sprite

Sounding rocket

Mysterious mesosphere

The mesosphere is hard to study because research balloons cannot reach it and satellite instruments find measuring it difficult. We do know that its sensitive gases respond to small changes in those from layers below. So further study might help us find more about the effects of increasing carbon gases released from Earth.

Night clouds

Very high night clouds, known as noctilucent clouds, occasionally illuminate the sky in the mesosphere, near Earth's poles. They are made of ice crystals that scatter light, making them shine. They occur in the freezing upper limit of this layer and are also known as Polar Mesospheric Clouds.

Night cloud

Lightning storm

Red sprites and elves

Long streaks of faint red light flash briefly above heavy storm clouds and lightning from the troposphere way below. A halo-shaped glow, or elve, forms above it (left). We do not know exactly why they form, but these fascinating lights are captured best by very sensitive, low light level television (LLLTV) equipment.

Airglow

The upper layers of the atmosphere give out very faint light the whole time. This is called airglow. Looking edge-on through the atmosphere from space, it makes a glowing band. Airglow is mostly caused by particles and radiation from the Sun affecting gases in the atmosphere in different ways.

Airglow

The Calm Stratosphere

The stratosphere can reach down to around 6 km (4 miles) and rise to its highest point around 50 km (30 miles) above Earth. These boundaries depend on the seasons and where you are in the world. They are also affected by electric storms in the troposphere below.

Mesosphere

Bright blue jets

Blue jets are narrow cones of pale blue lightning. They streak upwards from towering storm clouds in the troposphere below, moving at around 100 km/sec (60 miles/sec) – 300 times the speed of sound. They last just a fraction of a second.

Blue jet

Stratosphere

Troposphere

Storm cloud

Payload with instruments

Transporter

Studying weather

Every day, hundreds of huge weather balloons, 1.8 m (6 ft) in diameter, rise 32 km (20 miles) into the stratosphere. Each carries a radiosonde, which is a small bundle of instruments. These transmit data, such as temperature, pressure, wind speeds and heat radiation levels, to scientists, helping them to understand more about weather and climate.

Jetting high

Jet aircraft fly as much as possible in the lower part of the stratosphere, which is more stable than the stormy troposphere beneath it. The temperature in the stratosphere rises steadily and evenly with height, so hot and cold air mix less and there is less turbulence. Here, jet stream winds allow pilots to fly faster and save fuel.

Stable jet stream

Warm, moist air

Rain or snow

Bright nacreous cloud

Wavy clouds

Mother-of-pearl or 'nacreous' clouds in the stratosphere light up the evening sky with waves of rainbow colours, mostly at or towards the poles. They can be caused by winds much lower down, and occur at heights of around 20 km (13 miles). They are also known as winter Polar Stratospheric Clouds (PSCs).

The Ozone Layer

The protective ozone layer lies within the stratosphere around 16-38 km (10-24 miles) above the Earth. Ozone is a type of oxygen molecule that can absorb the most harmful, burning UV light from the Sun, which prevents most of it from reaching the ground.

Burning Earth

A thinning ozone layer allows more of the Sun's damaging UV rays to get through. These burn our skin and prevent plant growth, and also contribute to coral bleaching - killing off coral reefs.

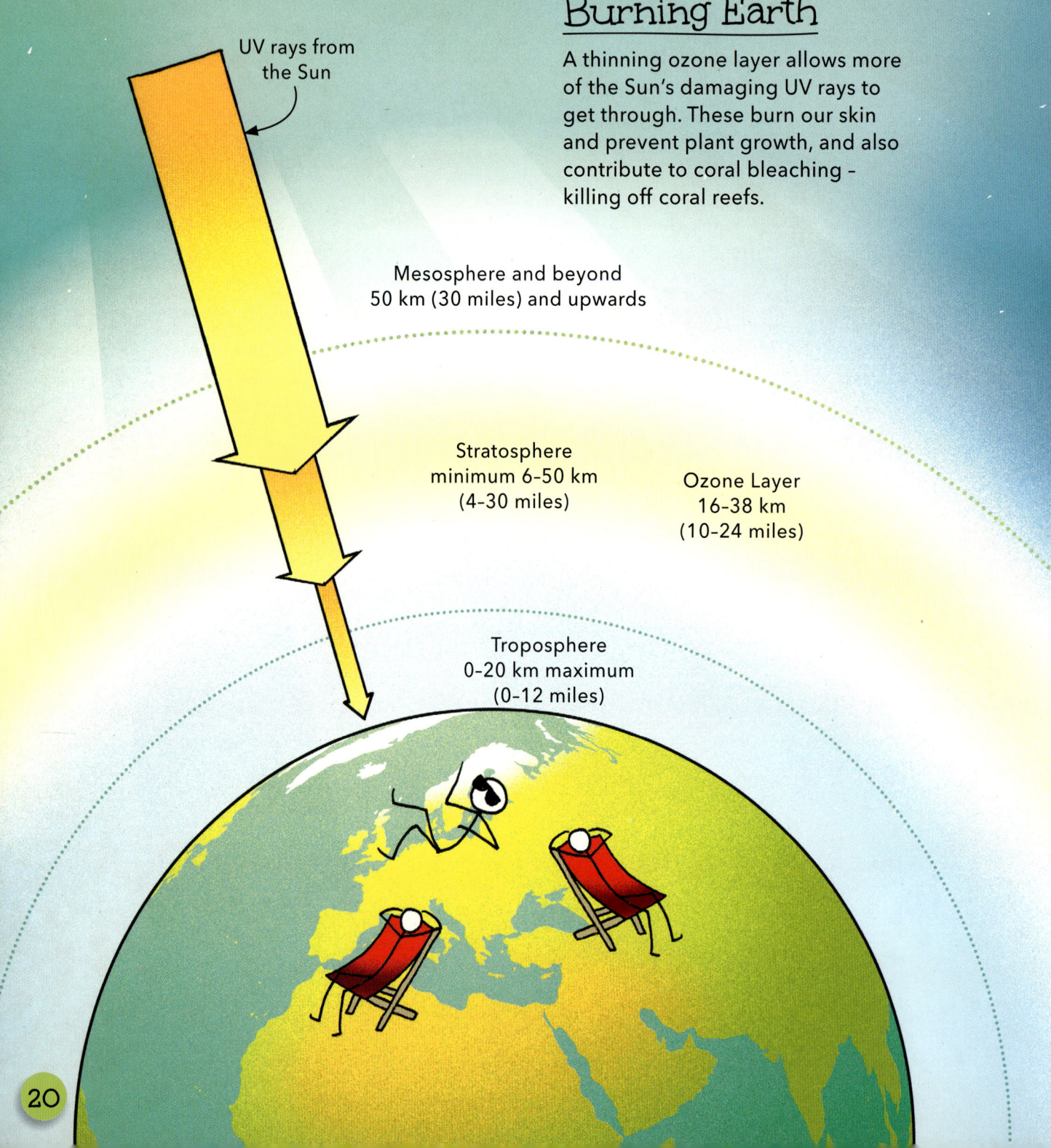

UV rays from the Sun

Mesosphere and beyond
50 km (30 miles) and upwards

Stratosphere
minimum 6-50 km
(4-30 miles)

Ozone Layer
16-38 km
(10-24 miles)

Troposphere
0-20 km maximum
(0-12 miles)

Damaging gases

In the 1980s, it was found that when gases called cholorfluorocarbons (CFCs) were exposed to the Sun's strong UV light, they released chlorine into the atmosphere. This caused the ozone layer to become thinner. So CFCs, which were used in aerosols, air conditioning units, refrigerators and insulating materials, were banned.

Thinning layer

The 'hole' in the ozone layer is actually a region where the layer is thinner, especially over the poles in springtime. It was discovered in the Antarctic in 1984 by the British scientist Joseph Farman, who used a ground-level instrument called the Dobson spectrophotometer, or Dobsonmeter. Now, thermal images from space satellites track the size and shape of the hole.

Measuring the ozone layer

A Dobsonmeter works out how much ozone there is absorbing the Sun's UV rays in the atmosphere. It was invented by the British meteorologist Gordon Dobson in the 1920s. Ozone levels in Antarctica reduced by about 50 percent in the worst years.

Earth's Troposphere

The troposphere is the layer that wraps immediately around the Earth's surface. It reaches from 0 km, or sea level, up to variable heights of 6-20 km (4-12 miles). It is the warmest layer, because Earth absorbs the Sun's warmth, then radiates it back up, heating the air near the ground.

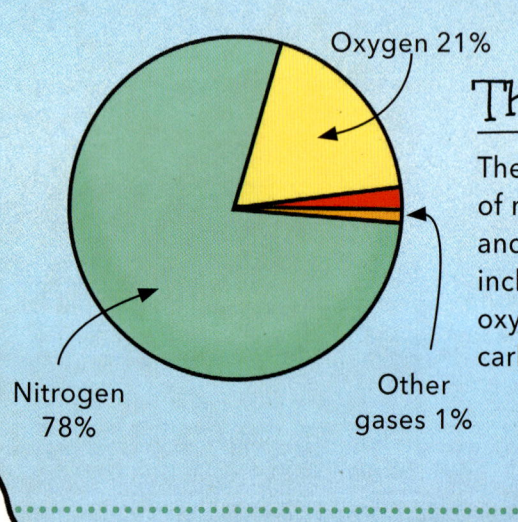

Oxygen 21%
Nitrogen 78%
Other gases 1%

The air we breathe

The troposphere is made up mainly of nitrogen with some oxygen and small amounts of other gases, including carbon dioxide. We need oxygen to breathe, and plants use carbon dioxide to grow.

Troposphere

Low air pressure
Air cools and thins as it rises
Mount Everest
Lightning storm
Precipitation (rain or snow)

A wavy layer

The upper boundary of the troposphere is not smooth but wavy. It is lowest over the poles and highest over the equator, reaching up to 20 km (12 miles). It is also lower in winter than summer. The top of the troposphere is very cold, because it lies far away from the Sun's radiated warmth nearer the ground and sea.

Thinner on top

Air gets thinner towards the top of the troposphere as air pressure drops. So there is less oxygen, which is why mountaineers usually carry oxygen supplies. This is also why aeroplane cabins are pressurized, providing the right oxygen levels and pressure for passengers and crew to breathe. Despite this, Rüppell's griffon vulture, one of the highest flying birds, has been recorded in flight at 10,900 m (36,000 ft) - even higher than an average commercial airliner.

Earth's water cycle

High in the troposphere, tall cloud columns rise. These form when the Sun heats up water from oceans and large lakes. The water evaporates from a liquid to a gas, which rises as it warms. High up, it cools and condenses into water droplets that form clouds. When the droplets are heavy enough, they fall as rain.

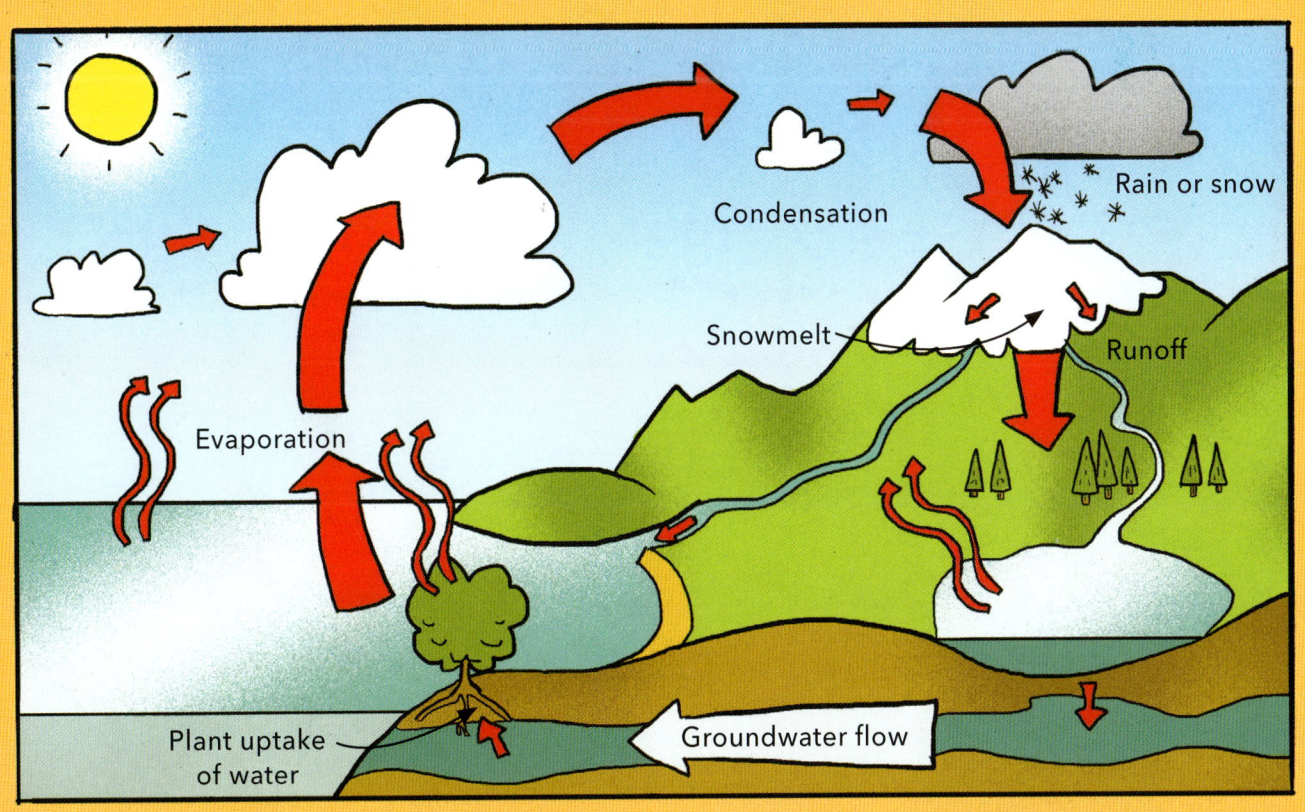

Storms and Twisters

Towering clouds in the troposphere bring strong winds, lashing rain and snow blizzards. The most destructive storms are called hurricanes, cyclones or typhoons, depending on where they blow. Twisting tornadoes suck up all that lies in their path.

Satellite

Hurricane in action

Storm motion

Clear, cloudless eye of storm

Weather balloon

Cold air

Warm, moist air

Warm updraught (upward air current)

Cold downdraught (downward air current)

Radar

Rain

Hurricanes from space

Satellites track the paths of hurricanes, which are wide banks of storm clouds rotating around a calm centre (called the 'eye'). Hurricanes develop over warm oceans, where winds pick up huge amounts of moist air. The moisture rises and forms clouds that are swirled around by driving winds. Hurricanes smack the land with destructive force and push up enormous waves, causing serious flooding.

Making rain

Climate change is making some regions on Earth drier. In some dry zones, rain clouds are artificially created. This is done by 'seeding' the air with chemicals. They draw together any water droplets in the air to form clouds. The chemicals can be spread by aircraft, or released by rockets and other launching equipment from the ground.

Twister!

Tornadoes blow along land, picking up warm moisture that rises until it hits very cold air at the top. This condenses it into tall, dark storm clouds. The clouds are blown by high-up winds from different directions, turning them into twisting, sucking storms that touch down in a funnel shape. Tornadoes can pick up houses, or even drop showers of frogs far away!

What's the Weather Like?

Weather encompasses the heat and cold, rain, snow, fog and wind that affect us every day on Earth. Observers at weather stations monitor temperature, humidity, wind speed and direction, and rain or snow fall on a daily and hourly basis. Their data is vital for making weather forecasts, ensuring people's safety and studying climate change.

What a wind!

Wind speeds can tell us how quickly a weather system, such as a storm, will reach us. They are measured with an anemometer, which captures the wind in rotating cups connected to an electric generator. This creates an electric current, which can be measured. A strong wind produces a high current.

Cups that rotate in the wind

Wind speed on LCD display

Handheld anemometer

Instrument case

Weather station

Up in the clouds

A ceilometer measures the height of clouds and visibility. It sends up invisible light beams that hit the base of a cloud. The beams are reflected back to Earth by the cloud, so the distance they travel can be calculated.

Ceilometer

How hot is it?

The first true thermometer for measuring temperature accurately was invented in 1724 by German physicist Gabriel Fahrenheit. He set a column of mercury, enclosed in glass, against a scale of measurement. Alcohol is now used instead of mercury, which is dangerous, while digital thermometers (right) are the latest technology, as well as safe. These may have a wireless sensor for use at a distance from the main unit. We still use degrees Fahrenheit as a temperature scale.

Digital thermometer

Wireless sensor for relaying temperature data to the receiver unit

Under pressure

Air pressure is the pressure exerted by the weight of air pushing down on Earth from above. It tells us roughly the type of weather we can expect for a few days. High air pressure usually brings clear skies and sunshine; low air pressure means rain, or a storm! Barometers measure air pressure.

Barometer

Hygrometer

Measuring humidity

We use a hygrometer to measure the air's moisture, or humidity. It tells us how much water vapour is in the air, and when it will form water droplets. This is important in such processes as applying paint coatings, and in conserving artworks and musical instruments.

27

Fantastic Sky Facts

Blue Moon

A truly blue Moon is a very rare sight. It only appears when huge amounts of smoke or dust particles are thrust high into the atmosphere, usually from volcanoes, allowing only blue light waves through. After the devastating eruption of the volcanic island of Krakatau in Indonesia in 1883, the Moon looked blue for months!

Crash!

More and more satellites are being launched into space. Over time, their orbits gradually change, so there is a risk of satellites crashing into each other. In 2009, two communication satellites collided for the first time. One was Russian and the other American, and both were destroyed.

Fast food delivery

How do astronauts on the ISS survive? Unmanned spacecraft called Automated Transfer Vehicles (ATVs) deliver fuel, food and science equipment. Scientists on Earth send a wide variety of foods to the astronauts. This is so that they can study the effect of each food on humans in weightless space.

Is there life out there?

The Hubble Space Telescope has been used to study the atmospheres of exoplanets – planets that orbit around other stars, just as Earth orbits around the Sun. About 2,000 exoplanets have been discovered and there could be billions of Earth-like planets in our Milky Way galaxy. But do they have life?

Fragile ozone layer

The ozone layer reacts quickly and strongly to extra chlorine gases. Just one chlorine atom can destroy more than 100,000 ozone molecules. Many extra chlorine and other harmful gases in the ozone layer are man-made. When they meet with high-rising gases from erupting volcanoes, they increase the damaging effect on the ozone layer.

Poisonous ozone!

Ten per cent of all ozone exists below the stratosphere. Here, ozone does not protect Earth from UV rays. Instead, it pollutes the air we breathe and can cause health problems. It also enters plant and crop systems, damaging growth. This ozone derives from industrial chemicals released into the air.

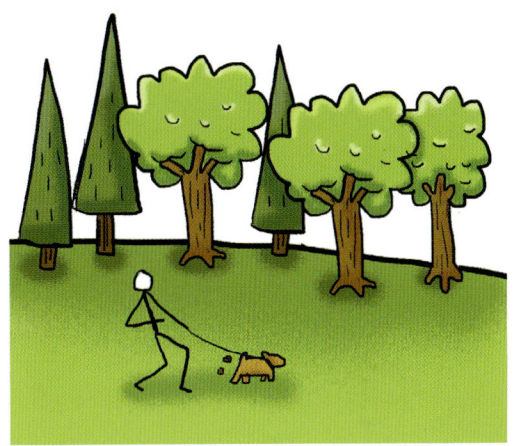

The worst hurricanes

Off the coast of Mexico in 2015, Hurricane Patricia's wind speed reached 325 km/h (200 mph), and it was declared the worst hurricane in history. Fortunately, there was no loss of life. On the other side of the Pacific in 2013, Typhoon Haiyan reached a wind speed of 315 km/h (195 mph). It hit the Philippines, killing 6,300 people. So the impact of a hurricane does not depend on wind speed alone.

Most terrible tornado

The worst tornado registered so far touched down on 18 March 1925. It twisted 480 km (300 miles) through Missouri, Illinois and Indiana – three states in what is known as Tornado Alley. It reached at least 415 km/h (260 mph), and 695 people died, with over 2,000 injured. Buildings were reduced to sticks and stones.

The Future...

The atmosphere's layers hold vital clues to the causes of climate change, as the Earth becomes warmer and sea levels rise. Studying our atmosphere has given scientists the tools to find out if we can survive on other planets...

Puzzling out climate change

The rate of Earth's temperature rise has doubled in the last 50 years. Is there a single cause, or several working together? Scientists study the gas types and movements in all Earth's layers to find out. They monitor greenhouse gases: carbon dioxide, methane and nitrous oxide, which hold in the Sun's heat as it radiates from Earth. The results, together with thermal images from satellites, and computer modelling, help to work out the future of our climate.

Other factors

The Sun's flares and sunspots may also be contributing to climate change. Scientists follow the Sun's effects on our planet, as Earth's distance from the Sun changes over a year and activity on the Sun varies. They are also looking in greater detail at the sources of pollution in our atmosphere. Small robotic drones hover over waste dumps to measure how much methane, a toxic gas, is rising skywards!

Life on Mars?

Since 2004, mobile robots called Rovers have been used on Mars to find out if the conditions there could ever have sustained life. The samples taken confirm that the atmosphere on Mars is now very thin, and that 95.3 per cent of it consists of carbon dioxide. Since 2012, the Rover 'Curiosity' has sent results proving that Mars once had surface water – one of the essential ingredients for life to exist.

Glossary

Comet
Small solar system object that grows tails of dust and gas when it gets near the Sun

Cyclone
Powerful rotating storm system

Galaxy
Large system of stars, dust and gas held together by gravity

Gravity
Attractive force that acts between all material things

Hypersonic
Speeds above five times the speed of sound

Infrared
Radiation similar to light but with longer wavelengths than visible light

Meteor
Small rock or dust particle from space burning up in the atmosphere as a streak of light in the sky

Orbit
Path followed by one body in space around another, such as a satellite around Earth

Radiation
A form of energy, such as light or X-rays, that can travel through empty space

Pressurized
Having a gas pressure inside that is greater than the pressure outside

Sounding rocket
Rocket carrying instruments that collect data or carry out experiments in space

Spectrograph
Instrument that separates and measures wavelengths of radiation

Ultraviolet
Invisible radiation similar to light, but more powerful and with shorter wavelengths

INDEX

A
air pressure 27
airglow 17
anemometers 26
astronauts 13, 28

B
barometers 27
blue jets 18
blue moons 28

C
ceilometers 26
chlorofluorocarbons (CFCs) 21
climate change 25, 30
clouds 17, 19, 23, 25, 26

D
Dobsonmeter 21

E
exosphere 6, 8–11

G
gases 9, 12, 16, 21, 22, 29, 30
geocorona 9
Global Positioning System (GPS) 10

H
Hubble Space Telescope 13, 14–15, 28
humidity 27
hurricanes 24–25, 29
hygrometers 27

I
International Space Station (ISS) 12, 13, 28

J
jet aircraft 19

M
Mars 30
mesosphere 6, 16–17

O
oxygen levels 23
ozone layer 20–21, 29

R
rain making 25
red elves 16, 17

S
satellites 10–11, 25, 28
sounding rockets 8

Southern Pinwheel galaxy 15
space shuttle 13
sprites and elves 17
storms 24–25, 29
stratosphere 6, 18–19
sun 9, 30

T
thermometers 27
thermosphere 6, 12–15
tornadoes 24, 25, 29
troposphere 6, 22–27

U
ultraviolet (UV) rays 9, 15, 20

W
water cycle 23
weather balloons 19
weather data 19, 26–27
wind speeds 26

X
X-15 rocket plane 13

The Author

Catherine Chambers was born in Adelaide, South Australia, grew up in the UK, and studied African History and Swahili at the School of Oriental and African Studies in London. She has written about 130 books for children and young adults, and enjoys seeking out intriguing facts for her non-fiction titles, which cover history, cultures, faiths, biography, geography and the environment.

The Illustrator

John Paul has a BSc in Biology from the University of Sussex, UK, and a graduate certificate in animation from the University of the West of England. He devotes his spare time to growing chilli peppers, perfecting his plan for a sustainable future and caring for a small plastic dinosaur. He has three pet squid that live in the bath, which makes drawing in ink quite economical …

Picture Credits (abbreviations: t = top; b = bottom; c = centre; l = left; r = right)
15 tr NASA, ESA, and the Hubble Heritage Team (STScI/AURA)